XANTHIPPE
a comedy

GREGORY EDWARD MANTELL

XANTHIPPE

ISBN: 979-8-9904606-4-5 (paperback)

ISBN: 979-8-9904606-5-2 (hardback)

ISBN: 979-8-9904606-6-9 (ebook)

ISBN: 979-8-9904606-7-6 (audiobook)

Cover and interior design: Andy Meaden meadencreative.com

*To My Family
Mom, Dad, Karen, and John*

CONTENTS

A NOTE TO LITERARY CRITICS EVERYWHERE

(Intelligent Readers Can Skip This Part)

Xanthippe is not a play about a shrew, or a taming of a shrew. It is, in fact, a comic dialog, an anti-dialog—a parody of Plato's Symposium and Plato's dialogs in general. (Without prompting the reader too much, I will merely point out that, among other things, Xanthippe and the Symposium both begin with Socrates standing in a trance on a porch, and both include a dinner party with Socrates and Aristophanes among the guests.) Moreover, by challenging Plato's portrayal of Socrates, Xanthippe seeks to raise a larger philosophical issue about the value of philosophy itself.

I believe the following quote by Allan Bloom will provide some insight into why I call Xanthippe a dialog rather than a play:

"(A) dialogue is ... neither poetry nor philosophy; it is something of both, but it is itself and not a mere

combination of the two. The fact that sometimes it does not meet the standards of the dramatic art reveals the same thing as the fact that sometimes the arguments are not up to the standards of philosophical rigor. The dialogue is the synthesis of these two polesand is an organic unity. Every argument must be interpreted dramatically, for every argument is incomplete in itself and only the context can supply the missing links. And every dramatic detail must be interpreted philosophically because these details contain the images of the problems which complete the arguments. Separately these two aspects are meaningless; together they are an invitation to the philosophic quest."

KANT ON LAUGHTER

" ... (A) joke must have something in it capable of momentarily deceiving us. Hence, when the semblance vanishes into nothing, the mind looks back in order to try it over again, and thus by a rapidly succeeding tension and relaxation it is jerked to and fro and put in oscillation. As the snapping of what was, as it were, tightening up the string takes place suddenly (not by gradual loosening), the oscillation must bring about a mental movement and a sympathetic internal movement of the body. This continues involuntarily and produces fatigue, but in so doing it also affords recreation (the effects of a motion conducive to health).

For supposing we assume that some movement in the bodily organs is associated sympathetically with all our thoughts, it is readily intelligible how the sudden act above referred to, of shifting the mind now to one standpoint and now to another, to enable it to contemplate its object, may involve a corresponding and reciprocal straining and slackening of the elastic parts of our intestines, which communicates itself to the diaphragm (and resembles that felt by ticklish people), in the course of which the lungs expel the air with rapidly succeeding interruptions, resulting in a movement conducive to health…"

—from the Critique of Judgment, Part II: Analytic of the Sublime

AUTHOR'S FOREWORD

If you like this work, I wish you well
If not, then you can go to ...

CHARACTERS

Xanthippe

Socrates

Apollodorus

Zenas

Morona

Antisthenes

Aristophanes

Agathon

Moderator

Lamphrocles

Alcibiades

SCENE I

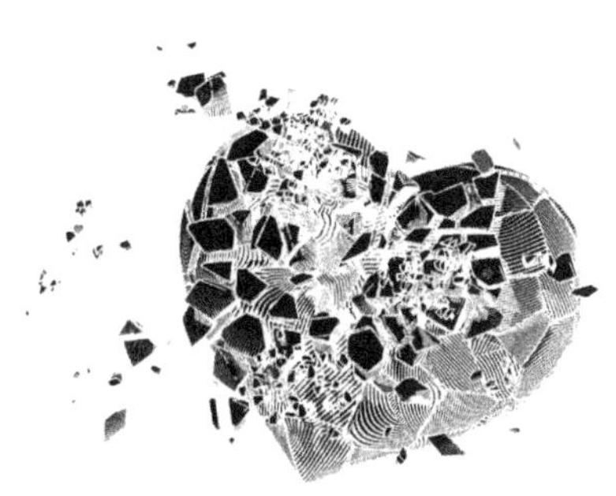

(A street in Athens. Socrates stands in a trance on a front porch at right. After a moment, two young Athenian men, Apollodorus and Zenas, enter from left. Apollodorus is a rogue and Zenas, his friend. Apollodorus, in particular, is good-looking.)

APOLLODORUS

The old man's really been giving me a hard time about coughin' up the dough this time. What does he expect me to do—get a job?!

ZENAS

I know—parents can be so unreasonable.

APOLLODORUS

I mean, he acts as though it's my fault the damn horse broke its leg right in the home stretch. How was I supposed to know that was going to happen when I made the bet?! Well, anyway, as the great Homer says, all's fair in love and war—which is definitely good advice for dealing with one's parents.

One way or another I'm gonna get the money out of him—even if I have to ....

(stops in midspeech and stares at Socrates, standing straight ahead of them on the porch; Socrates is barefoot and wearing a threadbare cloak.)

That has got to be the ugliest statue I have ever seen! How could somebody try to pass an eyesore like that off as a work of art?

ZENAS

That's not a statue, Apollodorus! That's Socrates—the wisest man in all of Greece.

APOLLODORUS

(waves his hand in front of his nose)

Pew! So that explains it! I wondered what that horrible smell was. They say he doesn't believe in taking a bath at least once a month like the rest of us.

ZENAS

It's not that he was raised in a barn.

It's just that his mind is occupied with more vapory, vacuous, philosophical things like being and becoming instead of vulgar, unimportant things like the body and bathing, that's all.

He's the guy who figured out that the truly wise man is he who knows he knows nothing. That's why the oracle at Delphi called him the wisest mortal alive.

APOLLODORUS

Well, it sounds like a fool's wisdom to me. So I guess that means every jackass you meet is a genius—or a philosopher.

ZENAS

No, no—you're missing the point. There's a difference between knowing nothing and KNOWING you know nothing.

APOLLODORUS

Oh, of course, I see. Silly me! Sort of like if you're stupid but you know you're stupid, then you're actually smart, huh?

ZENAS

Very funny. You just don't have the makings of a philosopher.

APOLLODORUS

Thank you!

But I know an old bum when I see one. And for somebody who doesn't know anything, they say he's pretty good at sniffing out all the best dinner parties.

And, by the way, where are his shoes? Oh, but I forgot —he probably doesn't need any; I suppose his head is so light with all those thoughts of the heavens it's full of, that he usually just floats along up in the clouds somewhere; he doesn't spend much time down here on earth.

And another thing—can you please tell me why he is just standing there like a damn bump on a log? I guess all that food and drink he sucked in at Alcibiades' must have temporarily grounded him. If he needs some assistance getting a move on it, I'll be happy to give him a little help. *(He kicks the air)*.

ZENAS

Don't you know anything?! You've been spending too much time at the law courts and the horse races. Everybody knows that every once in a while, Socrates gets so wrapped up thinking something really deep and awful that he just loses all touch with reality and goes off into his own little world somewhere.

Sometimes he just stands there all day—off in another dimension.

APOLLODORUS

You mean, Da Da Land? ...

(Zenas gives him a look that says he won't dignify Apollodorus' comment with a response.)

So, you're telling me that if I went over there and gave him a good slap upside the head, he wouldn't know what —or who—the hell hit him—literally.

ZENAS

Yes, exactly.

APOLLODORUS

Well, there's only one way to find out for sure. You wait right here.

(He begins to walk toward Socrates.)

ZENAS

Wait a minute, Apollodorus! You're not going to assault the greatest philosopher in all of Greece, are you?

(Apollodorus keeps walking; Zenas runs after him.)

Hey, wait up! Clinias wanted me to make sure Socrates was coming to his dinner tonight.

APOLLODORUS

(walking toward Socrates)

You don't have to worry about that—if there's free food and booze, you can be sure Socrates will be there.

It's easy to be poor and run around looking down on everybody else when you've got plenty of rich friends to leech off.

I don't buy this trance thing for one minute. These quacks'll do anything to make a name for themselves. He's a fraud and I'll prove it. I'll bring him back to reality!

(He makes as if to swing his arm at Socrates head.)

ZENAS

Apollodorus! For god's sake—don't! You'll kill him!

APOLLODORUS

All right, all right. Get a hold of yourself. I wasn't really going to hit him.

ZENAS

Yeah, sure.

APOLLODORUS

Be quiet—and watch this.

Eh, hem, pardon me, there, old man, sir, can you please tell me the way to the nearest brothel?

ZENAS

Apollodorus!

APOLLODORUS

All right—let me try something else.

(He grabs Socrates' nose; Socrates doesn't react.)

That's a mighty big nose you've got there, sir.

ZENAS

Apollodorus—stop it right now. Get away from him!

Besides, it's not going to do you any good. I told you—when he's philosophizing he's just like a zombie.

APOLLODORUS

He may have taken you all in, but he doesn't fool me. This guy's not off contemplating the universe somewhere; the only deep thoughts he's thinking are about who he can bum his next meal off.

Wait—I know how to get his attention!

(loudly)

Say, Zenas, my man, where's the party tonight? At Clinias'? And you did say Alcibiades is going to be there, right?

SOCRATES

(coming out of the trance)

Party? Alcibiades? Did somebody say something about a party and Alcibiades?

APOLLODORUS

(triumphantly)

See—what did I tell you?!

ZENAS

(under his breath, to Apollodorus)

Knock it off!

Socrates, I'm glad I found you here. I wanted to let you know about the party tonight at Clinias'. He wanted me to make sure you got his invitation.

SOCRATES

Thank you, Zenas, my fine young friend. Eating is good for the soul—or at least, it sure beats starving.

(turning toward Apollodorus)

And who, may I ask, is your fine, HANDSOME young friend?

ZENAS

This is Apollodorus, son of Callias.

SOCRATES

It is most definitely a pleasure to meet you. You are, indeed, your father's son—quite the picture of good health. I hope all is well with Callias. He and I used to have many conversations at the gym.

APOLLODORUS

Yes, he's warned me—I mean, told me—all about you.

ZENAS

(*intervening quickly*)

I've been trying to enlighten Apollodorus here by telling him all about your philosophy—about how you don't know anything, or, I mean, how you know you know nothing, er, well, um—you know!

(*with the sense that he's getting himself in deeper all the time*)

But he's skeptical. I don't think he's a philosopher at heart.

SOCRATES

Ah, Zenas, philosophy is concerned with the head, not the heart. The heart is the part of the body that has all the dense, warm blood in it. The head, however, is where the light, airy thoughts swirl around.

APOLLODORUS

Speaking of airy, it does seem a bit windy all of a sudden.

ZENAS

(hits Apollodorus discreetly; mumbles under his breath)

Shut up!

SOCRATES

Afterall, it's a well known fact that people tend not to philosophize as much when their heads have been removed.

APOLLODORUS

(speaks so that only Zenas hears)

Don't give me any ideas, old man.

(Zenas hits him again).

SOCRATES

Not everyone is cut out for the study of philosophy. Just a select few. Maybe we can talk it over more at dinner tonight, my fine, vigorous-looking young man. Maybe I can convert you.

All I know is I know nothing, which I'll prove to you if you talk to me long enough.

APOLLODORUS

So I've heard. But I do think I've pretty much mastered the main part of your philosophy. Is there anything more to it than that—just being ignorant?

SOCRATES

My basic philosophy routine—for dinner parties, of course!—is first I prove I don't know anything.

Then I prove you don't know anything.

And then—if the wine holds out—I prove that nobody knows anything. And if it turns into a really riotous, drunken brawl, I pull out all the stops and drink everybody under the table discussing virtue.

ZENAS

What's amazing is, nobody's ever seen Socrates drunk. No matter how much he drinks—even if he's been at it all night—he's just as sharp as ever and can outargue anyone.

APOLLODORUS

Yes, I've wondered about that. How exactly is it, Socrates, that you remain so completely in control, even if you drink enough to kill a horse, or two?

Is it because of your philosophy?

SOCRATES

(bashful)

Well, no, my young friend, it's just that over the years I've developed—

APOLLODORUS

A high tolerance?

ZENAS

But what amazes me even more than his ability to out-slosh the biggest lushes who've ever lived is his ability to withstand Alcibiades' charms. If you don't mind my mentioning it, Socrates, even Alcibiades admits he's never had any luck with you.

(to Apollodorus)

At one of Agathon' s party not that long ago Alcibiades told everybody about how he made a pass at Socrates once but Socrates completely ignored him. Alcibiades thought that just because he was so good-looking he could seduce Socrates without any effort, if he really wanted to. So he waited one night 'til after dinner when everyone else had left, and he and Socrates were alone. It was during the winter, so Alcibiades seized on that as a pretense for putting his cloak around Socrates and holding him in his arms, saying he just wanted to keep him warm—which, by the way, I think would have been pretty thoughtful of him if it had been true.

But, anyway, Alcibiades was sure Socrates would try something if he did that. But even though Alcibiades held him all night, when the next morning came and it was time for Socrates to leave, nothing more had happened than if they had been brothers sleeping together.

APOLLODORUS

I'm glad I'm not in your family! But I agree—that certainly is a very unusual display of denial and self-control.

I mean, it must have been very hard to allow one of the best-looking men in all of Greece to hold you tight in a bear hug all night and not just get up and walk away.

Sounds as though he's got the old 'hard-to-get' routine down pretty well.

XANTHIPPE

(screaming from offstage)

Socrates! I see you there! Where have you been hiding all day! Just wait until I get my hands on you.

SOCRATES

Holy Zeus, it's Xanthippe! She's found me! Well, gentlemen, I've really enjoyed our little chat but my inner voice tells me its time to run—I mean hide—I mean—Good-bye!

APOLLODORUS

(glances at Socrates as he runs off, then turns toward Zenas)

He sure hightailed it out of here pretty fast. That doesn't seem very philosophical to me. What happened to his otherworldly detachment?

ZENAS

You'd be scared, too, if you had a wife like that. Oh, no, here she comes.

XANTHIPPE

(enters)

Where did that no good Socrates sneak off to! I saw him standing here talking some more of his damn nonsense!

APOLLODORUS

He took off in a hurry—like a witch was after him—in that direction!

(points upward)

XANTHIPPE

I'll come back and scratch your eyes out later, my smart-mouthed young man.

(hurries off in the direction Socrates went)

ZENAS

You'd better watch it. Believe me, you don't want Xanthippe on your case!

APOLLODORUS

I'll take my chances. So tell me, why did he marry her anyway, if she's so hard to get along with. Did they have to?

ZENAS

No, of course not!

Why does anybody get married? I guess he's a glutton for punishment.

My parents fight all of the time, too. Don't yours? I think that's what married people are supposed to do.

Socrates does seem to get a bit of a raw deal, though. Usually a marriage is pretty much a toss up. The wife fights with her mouth, and the husband with his hands. So it's pretty much an even battle. But Xanthippe does both—first she nags him, then she beats him.

APOLLODORUS

Well, if he lets her do it, he's only got himself to blame.

SCENE II

(Marketplace. Socrates runs in full speed ahead, glancing backward to see "how he's doing." He collides with a booth set up by a mask maker.)

ANTISTHENES

Hey, watch where you're going, buddy! Open your damn eyes! What's the big idea—running through here like a maniac!

SOCRATES

(frantic)

I'm sorry, Antisthenes, but you've got to help me.

ANTISTHENES

Socrates—It's you!

My god—I'm sorry! I mistook you for another one of those damn beggars that keeps plaguing us. The markets full of 'em.

But what is it? What's the matter?

SOCRATES

Xanthippe's after me. She's hot on the trail and hot on my tail! I can't let her find me.

If she catches me, she'll skin me alive, and then I won't be able to go to Clinias' party tonight. You've got to help.

XANTHIPPE

(offstage)

Socrates!

ANTISTHENES

Here, quick! Put this on and don't say a word.

(hands Socrates a donkey's mask)

Just stand there and keep quiet.

XANTHIPPE

(enters running, bellowing)

Socrates! Now where did that damn bum go! I know I saw him go this way. He can run but he can't hide. I know all his usual hangouts. And it's just going to go harder on him when I do find him.

(talks to Antisthenes, but throws a quick but suspicious glance at Socrates, in disguise, standing near him)

Pardon me, sir, did you happen to notice a big rat just come running through here in the past few minutes?

ANTISTHENES

Nope, didn't see a thing. No rats around here, ma'am. Not one all day.

XANTHIPPE

In this part of town! That's a lie! You must be hiding something!

ANTISTHENES

Well, all right, then,
Since you're so bold
If the truth be told
I've seen so many
I can't remember any

XANTHIPPE

Ah, very good, but...
If you value your life
Listen to what I say
Lie to an angry wife
And it's judgment day

ANTISTHENES

I can't make any promises. But, all right, tell me, what did this rat look like?

XANTHIPPE

Well, for starters, it's about six feet tall.

ANTISTHENES

By all that's holy! That's bigger than the most giantesque sewer rat I've ever heard of! I'm sure I would have noticed something like that if it had gone by.

But I'd better be sure; I'm scared to ask, but is there anything else I should know about it?

XANTHIPPE

Let's see—It has white hair and is about sixty years old and could talk your ear off spouting a lot of damn fool nonsense about philosophy.

ANTISTHENES

Good god, lady—that's not a rat you're talking about! That's a damn demon or a freak of nature you're describing!

Are you sure you maybe haven't been hitting the bottle just a bit?

XANTHIPPE

(in a rage)

Am I sure! I'll say—I'm married to him!

ANTISTHENES

Please, lady, don't say another word. I don't want to hear it. This is a respectable establishment we're running here.

Let's just pretend you never brought up the subject. I, for one, promise I won't tell anybody.

XANTHIPPE

Look, buddy. You can cut the crap right now. I saw my husband come this way and I know he's got to be around here somewhere.

In fact, I wouldn't be surprised if you're hiding him.

(eyes Socrates again)

You know, that jackass sure looks familiar.

ANTISTHENES

(quickly)

Oh, that—that's not for sale. It's just on display. It's for Aristophanes' new play. He's already bought it. He's picking it up tomorrow.

Maybe I could interest you in one of these other masks. One of these gorgons would suit you perfectly. How 'bout Medusa here?

XANTHIPPE

(musing)

So Aristophanes has another play coming out, does he, the drunk? Well, if he needs an ass's mask, it must be another one about my husband—I'm ruined!

One more play by Aristophanes about Socrates and his damn stupidity and it'll be the end of me. I was the laughingstock of the town after that last one, The Clouds, came out. All the women in the market place made fun of me, saying every nasty thing they could think of, about how I had a lunatic, numskull of a husband who flew around in baskets like a madman.

And what was worse was—I had to agree with 'em!

Maybe I should destroy this jackass before Aristophanes gets his hands on it.

(Socrates sneezes.)

XANTHIPPE

(triumphantly)
Sir, I believe your mannequin just sneezed.

That must be a very remarkable dummy.

ANTISTHENES

What do you mean, sneeze? I didn't hear anything.

(Xanthippe hits "the donkey" hard.)

SOCRATES

Ouch!

XANTHIPPE

And it talks, too!

ANTISTHENES

I didn't hear anything. I think your imagination is getting the best of you.

XANTHIPPE

I know an ass when I hear one, and I'll be damned if that didn't sound exactly like my husband! *(She slugs him again and tries to take the mask off, but Socrates holds it on; as they struggle ...).* Now your dummy's fighting me. It must be possessed. I'd better kill it!

ANTISTHENES

(aside)

I wouldn't want to be in old Socrates shoes right now—if he had any.

(After a struggle, Xanthippe succeeds in pulling the mask off.)

ANTISTHENES

(aside)

Ah, oh—busted.

SOCRATES

What is it, Xanthippe, my little sweet pea?

XANTHIPPE

Don't 'sweet pea' me, you old monster!

Where have you been all day? Off gallivanting all over town again with your fancy friends!

And I suppose you've got another one of your banquets lined up for tonight—while your wife and children are home eating somebody else's scraps I scrounged up from the garbage piles at the market.

SOCRATES

It's good not to waste food.

(Xanthippe hits him violently, while he tries to fend her off; during the following speech, she alternates between beating him up and sobbing pitifully.)

XANTHIPPE

Don't give me any more of your damn lessons on economizing! I already make a church mouse look extravagant. Save 'em for all your big-spender friends!

(She bursts into tears but continues to slap him.)

I don't know any other woman who would put up with this.

(registers a good hit)

I just let you walk all over me.

(hits him a few more times as she sobs)

Nobody else would be stupid enough to let you take advantage of 'em the way I do.

My father warned me about marrying a philosopher. He told me I'd regret it, but I didn't believe him. When I heard how much Gorgias and all the others were charging their students, I thought you'd really rake it in like the rest of 'em.

Everybody said you could out-babble 'em all. But I was a fool! I married the only philosopher dumb enough to blab it all away for nothing!

What would I care if you spent all day talking to every idiot in town who was dumb enough to listen—if you could make a buck doing it!

But—no—you can't stop those gums from flapping in the breeze in the direction of anybody who'll look your way—free of charge!

No—you couldn't take a dime from anybody because you're too damn good to earn a honest living like everybody else!

Well, let me tell you something—you're wife and children are the ones who really have to pay the price for all of your fancy philosophy talk!

(breaks down, sobbing)

(Socrates, who thinks she has weakened sufficiently, begins to slowly back up, as though he's going to try to make off while the going's good.)

XANTHIPPE

(flies into a fury again)

Where do you think you're sneaking off to, old man!
she grabs a hold of his cloak and tears most of it off)

There—now you can go run and hide!
(screaming and crying)

I just can't take it any more!

Get away from me! Leave me alone!

(She runs off).

ANTISTHENES

That's some wife you've got there.

SOCRATES

Do be quiet.

ANTISTHENES

Why do you let her hit you like that?

Any day I'd let some woman attack me—I'd send her flying!

SOCRATES

What? Did you want me to get into a boxing match with her right here?

(mimicking)

That's one for Xanthippe—oh, there's one for Socrates!

Do you want it to be the talk of Athens how Socrates beat up his wife in the marketplace?

ANTISTHENES

You don't have to worry about that, Socrates—we all know who the one getting beat up is. Here, let me give you a cloak to put over yourself.

SCENE III

(Xanthippe is scrubbing the floor in a room of the house while her son Lamphrocles runs around holding a bowl as a toy.)

XANTHIPPE

Lamphrocles, I already told you once and I'm not going to tell you again, young man. Put that down before you break it!

(She keeps on cleaning and he keeps on running. He trips and drops the bowl, and starts crying.)

XANTHIPPE

(she "stands up" on her knees)

Now see what you've done! I told you to put that thing down before you broke it!

Now go to your room this instant, young man, and don't come out until I tell you you can!

LAMPHROCLES

But I didn't mean to break it, Mommy.

XANTHIPPE

Go to your room this instant! Young brats who don't listen to their mothers don't need supper! You're going to grow up to be just like your worthless father!

LAMPHROCLES

(running off)

I hate you—I hate you! I wish you were dead!

XANTHIPPE

Lamphrocles—get back her right now, young man, and apologize!

(She slides down into a semi-seated position and breaks down crying.)

MORONA

(enters, hesitatingly)

Xanthippe, are you all right? If this is a bad time, I can come back later.

XANTHIPPE

(stands up; she slowly regains her spirits the more she talks)

Morona, I don't know how much longer I can put up with this.

It's the same thing everyday—Socrates out on the town from morning 'til night, living it up with his rich friends, while the kids and I are stuck in this dump.

He's a regular socialite; hardly an evening goes by when he hasn't gotten an invitation from another one of his no good friends who doesn't have anything better to do than get drunk every night.

Well, I'm sick and tired of it! Do you know how hard it is to try to make a decent meal when there's no food in the house?

Now the kids are starting to resent me because I'm the one who has to discipline them all the time since there father's never around.

And do you know how long it's been since I've had a new dress? I've been wearing this same damn rag since the day we were married. I never have anything new and pretty to wear to any of the festivals like all the other women.

Whenever some rich old hag wants to put somebody down, she says, "Where'd she get that potato sack? She looks like the wife of Socrates!"

MORONA

Personally I've never understood how you've been able to put up with things as long as you have. I would have murdered him a long time ago.

XANTHIPPE

I've been trying to think of a way to come up with some money—since I can't count on my husband for anything. But I can't think of anything realistic.

I thought about becoming a housebreaker, but I don't know what would happen to my kids if I got caught.

I even thought about setting up shop in the market place, but the problem is I don't know what I could do or sell.

I'm no damn good at fortune telling—except for predicting my own future, which doesn't look very good—and weaving and basketmaking have never been my strong points.

MORONA

Arts and crafts are a decent enough way to make a living, to be sure, but there are other older, more profitable professions.

XANTHIPPE

You don't mean ... pro ... pros ... sti ...

(*chokes on word*)

(begins to consider it seriously for half a second, upbeat)

Hey, do you really think I. ?

(serious again)

But what would my children think if they found out their mother was a... a... a ....

MORONA

Tramp, harlot, slut, whore.

XANTHIPPE

(dryly)

Thank you.

MORONA

Who says you have to tell them? We all have our little secrets.

XANTHIPPE

I wouldn't! But someone else would!

MORONA

Well, it's just an idea. I'm only trying to help.

XANTHIPPE

I know. Oh, what am I going to do?

MORONA

We'll think of something.

(pauses, thinking)

O.k., let's take stock of the situation. The way I see it—you've got three options—you can either leave him, sue him, or kill him.

XANTHIPPE

But I can't leave him - where would I go? I can't go home.

My father's wedding present to me was this advice: "You can marry that damn bum if you want to, but when you finally figure out how worthless he is don't come running home here crying to me."

Which naturally only made me want to marry him all the more at the time.

MORONA

You could always go abroad.

XANTHIPPE

What, and raise my children like beggars in a foreign country!

MORONA

Well, that still leaves two options.

XANTHIPPE

Then I've got no choice at all—It's not worth killing him for the same reason it's not worth suing him—he doesn't have any money.

MORONA

(dispirited)

Good point.

(thinks hard).

Wait, I've got it!

XANTHIPPE

What?

MORONA

Well, you know what they say—if you can't beat 'em, join 'em!

XANTHIPPE

What do you mean? What do you want me to do?

Abandon my kids every night and start tagging along with him at those drunken parties at Alcibiades'?

MORONA

Of course not.

What I mean is—turn the tables on him and use his philosophy against him.

Challenge him to a public debate and put his reputation on the line.

Then, when he loses he'll be so humiliated he'll have to give up philosophizing forever. In other words, if you can't join 'em—beat 'em!

XANTHIPPE

(thinks it over; excitedly)

That's a great idea. It's perfect, as a matter of fact.

(looses steam)

But what if he won't agree to do it?

MORONA

Believe me, he'll agree. He knows that if he doesn't, you can make his life a living hell.

XANTHIPPE

But I thought I already DO make his life a living hell.

MORONA

Yes, you do. And that's why it's in his best interest to agree to this debate. He's got nothing to lose and much to gain—namely peace and quiet.

If he wins, you'll agree to stop hounding him about philosophy and let him spend all the time he wants to babbling to his friends.

XANTHIPPE

But what if I lose?

MORONA

Then things will stay pretty much just the same, since that's what he does right now. I don't see how things could get much worse.

XANTHIPPE

You're right! But do you really think I can pull it off?

I mean, they say he's pretty good. You know what Aristophanes said—about how he can make the Worse Argument defeat the Better.

They say he can make mincemeat of the most petty, low-life, slippery-tongued, weaselly lawyer you'd ever meet.

MORONA

Of course. He's much worse than a lawyer—he's a philosopher.

XANTHIPPE

But even Athena herself, then, wouldn't have a chance in Hades against him, and I'm just a country girl.

MORONA

Don't worry—you're underestimating yourself, Xanthippe. You've got an even bigger advantage.

XANTHIPPE

What! Please tell me!

MORONA

You're mouth! All wives are naturally gifted at outarguing their husbands.

Don't tell me you didn't know that! If you claim otherwise, that's an assault upon our sex. What, were you an orphan child?

Didn't your mother scold and nag your father all the time?

XANTHIPPE

Yes.

MORONA

And didn't she worry him and wear down his nerves until he was practically a walking vegetable?

XANTHIPPE

Yes, but he deserved it.

MORONA

There—now you're coming around! That's the spirit!

Just remember, while Socrates is preparing himself for the debate by getting all calm and philosophical and detached, you work yourself up into a fury and let nature take its course.

Just pretend he was out all night at a party and you were trapped at home and think of how upset would be.

Just get yourself all emotional and crazy—really let yourself go wild. That should do the trick no problem.

In fact, I think I'm starting to pity the poor guy.

XANTHIPPE

(as she talks she becomes increasingly furious)

But he WAS out all night, that no good bum. Not that that's anything new, of course. I'm always at home slaving away, being the man and the woman of the house, while he's off partying all over town with his damn friends.

He can talk up a storm with all his fine talk about being a good person. But if he's such a good husband and a father, why are his wife and kids running around in rags wondering where their next meal's going to come from?

MORONA

Trust me—he doesn't have a prayer!

You're gonna blow him out of the water. Do half as well tomorrow—and your husband can kiss his days as a philosopher good-bye!

SCENE IV

(Socrates enters in the dark. Xanthippe has booby-trapped the door with pots and pans. Socrates trips and stumbles.)

SOCRATES

The heavens above! Murdered in the night! Evil is the world in which we live. Much better is the place to which I go.

XANTHIPPE

(comes rushing into the room after all the clatter)

What in the hell is going on in here? Who's making all that racket?

If it's a burglar, you have definitely come to the wrong house; there's nothing worth stealing in this rundown shack.

In fact, if you don't get out of here right now, I may rob you ....

Oh, Socrates, it's you. Sorry—I must have forgot to put those pots and pans away.

SOCRATES

A man is lucky who has a loving wife to come home to.

XANTHIPPE

Don't give me any of your wisecracks, buddy! A man who comes traipsing in at the crack of dawn every day is lucky he has a wife who hasn't killed him.

It's nice of you to sneak in and grace your wife and children with your presence while they're sleeping.

No doubt all your talk did a lot to improve the morals of your damn drinking buddies—before they all passed out!

Are you plastered? How many fingers am I holding up?

(makes her hand into a fist and holds in his face)

SOCRATES

Xanthippe, you'll wake the children if you continue on like this. Let's do call it a night.

XANTHIPPE

Don't try to use little kids to protect yourself, you overgrown coward!

My talking won't wake the children—although an old man's screams for help might!

I can tell you one thing, though—I'm not putting up with this for one more day. I'm putting an end to things once and for all tonight!

SOCRATES

By Apollo, it's wrong to take your own life, Xanthippe. The gods don't approve of suicide. And your children wouldn't have anyone to take of them!

XANTHIPPE

If I kill anyone—it won't be me, you worthless old bum.

If you were smart, you'd be more worried about saving your own life instead of mine.

SOCRATES

If you wish to discuss anything in a way that will tend to improve either one of us, Xanthippe, I will be happy to indulge you; if not, I really must be going to bed.

I must say I do feel a bit fatigued after exerting myself so strenuously eating and talking all night.

XANTHIPPE

I should break your damn neck after that little stunt you pulled in the market today!

You're just lucky I'm such a pushover, you old bastard, or I would have killed you a long time ago! But fortunately, I'm not the kind of person who holds grudges—damn you!

I believe in rising above things! The fact that you're still breathing proves it!

But for once in your fool life you finally said something that had an ounce of sense in it. A talk is exactly what I want—in fact, a debate would be more like it.

I want to have it out once and—for all, like a civilized, rational person.

I want to see whether you're as good with all your flaky philosophy as you claim you are.

SOCRATES

I don't think I heard you correctly; I thought I just heard you say you wanted to have a rational discussion for a change.

Either something is wrong with my ears, or I'm afraid you must have hurt yourself while I was out today.

Please don't take this the wrong way, but did you fall and hit your head when I was gone, Xanthippe?

But please don't let me interrupt; please do feel free to continue.

XANTHIPPE

I guess being married to Mr. Smooth Talker has finally rubbed off on me.

What, are you scared your wife will make you look like a fool in front of the whole city?

SOCRATES

They say if you live long enough you'll see and hear it all, and it must be true!

But the gods above! Who would have thought that at my age there was something like this waiting to spring on me around the bend! Xanthippe, a philosopher!

By Zeus! I'm absolutely thunderstruck! Never in my wildest dreams—and believe me, I've had some pretty wild dreams, especially after some of those parties at Alcibiades!

Perhaps I've underestimated you this past decade, my little tulip. Truly, Xanthippe, never more during our marriage have I felt more like giving you a hug and a kiss.

(makes as if to approach her to give her a hug and a kiss)

XANTHIPPE

Don't you come near me, you old lech! I mean it—or I'll throttle you with my bare hands. Don't go getting all excited at your parties and then come home here all hot to trot!

SOCRATES

You can roar like a lion if you will, my little apple dumpling, but the sound of your sweet voice will always be music to my ears.

I agree wholeheartedly to this debate. I'm absolutely astounded! Here I've been wondering around this city all these years, like a dolt, eagerly looking for anyone to take on as an opponent, and yet all this time, right under my very nose, was my own darling little wife, waiting to be

my next victim, er, urn, opponent, or, urn ....

I am more than willing to discuss with you any thing you want in a public forum, Xanthippe.

XANTHIPPE

But there are certain terms and conditions.

SOCRATES

Now this is beginning to sound more like the Xanthippe I know.

XANTHIPPE

As I'm sure you'll agree there isn't room enough under this roof for more than one philosopher. Everybody knows that if you put two philosophers together in a room, let alone a house, there's certain to be a war or death, what with all of their damn quibbling and nonsense.

So whichever one of us happens to lose has to agree to give up philosophizing, at least if they want to continue living or remain in this house. And the one who wins can do all of the damn philosophizing they want to wherever they want to whenever they want to, without any interference from the other.

Agreed?

SOCRATES

I don't know what this means—perhaps the end of the world! But it's an omen from above—a blessed miracle!

You are indeed correct, my little darling. Considering how much having one philosopher in the house has been conducive to domestic harmony, I don't think any of us could survive for long with another around, so I accept your terms and conditions.

But there is one more detail, who is to judge this contest? Who shall determine the winner?

XANTHIPPE

Anyone or his brother—what in the Hades do I care who it is that decides you're a damn fool. Anyone in Athens can come to that conclusion.

SOCRATES

The truly wise man does not heed the decision of the rabble. He follows the truth as it appears to his own soul. He uses his own mind and reason to arrive at the way things really are and should be. Then, even if the whole town be against him, he has obeyed the most important voice, and has acted correctly.

Therefore, I'm afraid I can't agree to abide by the decision of just anyone, only a wise man. If anyone other than a sage chooses the winner, then I will be forced to rely on my own judgment to determine the outcome and the true victor of our contest.

XANTHIPPE

Listen, buddy—you've been judge and jury long enough. Now we're going to give somebody else a turn.

Let me impart some wisdom to your soul: There are two ways you can participate in this debate—the easy way or the hard way.

Either you'll get up there on the platform using your own two feet, or I'll drag you up there kicking and screaming! Get the picture?

Good!

SCENE V

(Street in Athens. Apollodorus is walking along, when Zenas rushes upon him from behind, excited.)

ZENAS

Apollodorus, where have you been? I've been looking for you all afternoon. Did you hear the news?

APOLLODORUS

I've been running errands and had appointments all day. What news?

Oh, yeah, about your friend, the philosopher. It's all over town about how his charming wife gave him a pretty good drubbing in the market place—again.

ZENAS

No, that's old news—I mean, the latest news.

APOLLODORUS

My god, she finally killed him! Yippee! I made a huge bet with Aristademus about that a while ago.

(ecstatic, shouts)

Yes! By Zeus—that's the best news I've had all day! Now I don't have to worry about that damn horse racing debt anymore! I have to run and get my money!

ZENAS

No, that's not it! She didn't kill him, for god's sake!

APOLLODORUS

(disappointed)

She didn't?

ZENAS

No! She challenged him to a debate tomorrow at the town center. And listen to this—if she wins, he's agreed to give up philosophy.

If he wins, she's promised to stop being such an unbearable old hag. Everybody's gonna be there—the whole town!

APOLLODORUS

I can imagine. They're probably hoping it'll turn into another one of their brawls. (suddenly, excited)

Hey, maybe she'll do him in yet! Maybe right there at the debate tomorrow!

ZENAS

You're hopeless. But come on! Follow me! Agathon is having a party tonight for Socrates—a pre-victory celebration.

APOLLODORUS

Isn't that just a bit premature?

ZENAS

Not at all. You don't really think she'll win, do you! But we want to do everything we can to help cheer Socrates on to victory.

The dinner's probably over by now, but the after dinner drinking and philosophy should just be getting started. Come on—let's go!

APOLLODORUS

O.k., o.k.

SCENE VI

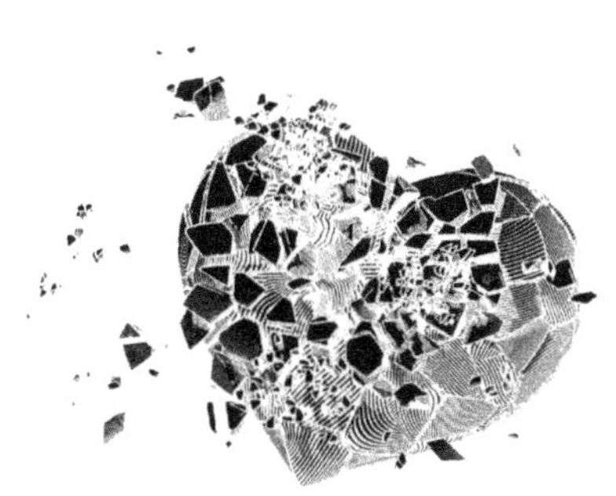

(Agathon's place. A servant announces Apollodorus and Zenas' arrival as they enter the dinner party, a small group of mostly young men. Aristophanes and Socrates are present as well.)

AGATHON

Ah, look who's here everyone—Apollodorus and Zenas!

(They exchange general greetings.)

We had all just about given up on you two! Now Alcibiades is the only one we're missing. Come—do come sit over here by Socrates and me.

SOCRATES

Yes, do.

ZENAS

(as he and Apollodorus walk to their couches)

I hope you'll agree this is a case of better late than never.

AGATHON

Certainly, it's good to see you both.

SOCRATES

Yes, two handsome young men like yourselves will definitely make an excellent addition to our little gathering here.

APOLLODORUS

In that case, maybe I should say I hope you didn't miss us too much.

AGATHON

Well, obviously, you've heard the big news.

ZENAS

How couldn't we! That's all everyone's been talking about. Is it true, Socrates—you'd really give up philosophy?

SOCRATES

Well, that's the deal, at any rate, though I won't comment on the likelihood of such a conclusion to the event. But I will, of course, abide by the terms, however the debate turns out.

After all, if I'm such a poor philosopher that I can't hold my own against Xanthippe, then I've taken up the wrong cause; I shouldn't be making it my life's work to go around claiming to enlighten all of the attractive young men in this city.

AGATHON

(to Apollodorus and Zenas)

Well, as you know, gentlemen, this isn't just another one of our friendly little drinking bouts. In light of today's events I have decided to hold this emergency dinner party with Socrates here as our guest of honor.

And in keeping with the spirit of the occasion, we decided before you got here to forego our usual method of entertaining ourselves—drinking ourselves blind— to help make sure that Socrates isn't forced into early retirement.

Not that there's much of a chance of that happening, of course!

GROUP

Hear, hear!

ZENAS

I propose a toast, gentlemen. To Socrates, the greatest philosopher of our time.

GROUP

To Socrates.

ARISTOPHANES

Bottoms up.

AGATHON

As I was saying, to help Socrates prepare for the big debate tomorrow we have asked him to hold a sort of practice exercise for the benefit of all of us here tonight.

Have you decided yet, Socrates, what subject you will take up for our enlightenment?

SOCRATES

Since you are our host tonight, Agathon, I will leave that decision up to you.

AGATHON

Very well, then, Socrates. The presence of so many of Athen's finest here tonight inspires me, and since love is the one subject even you profess to be an expert on, I propose that be the topic of our, or your, discussion—the nature of love.

SOCRATES

You are right, my friend—that is indeed the one subject I claim to have any special knowledge of and so....

ARISTOPHANES

Not so fast, Socrates old boy!

(to everyone)

I object—since we all owe our dinner tonight and entertainment tomorrow to our distinguished guest's marital bliss, I propose that in honor of his extraordinary wife—yes, I mean Xanthippe, in case you're all wondering who I'm talking about—I propose that that particular form of love known as marriage be the subject of Socrates' talk.

(Everyone laughs.)

AGATHON

Very well, then. This isn't a court of law, Aristophanes, but your objection is duly noted and approved. That is, as long as Socrates agrees.

SOCRATES

Agreed.

APOLLODORUS

Marriage—now that's a subject you should really have special expertise about, Socrates.

SOCRATES

Expertise, no. Nightmares, yes. But remember, my young friend, your day is coming as well. It's every young man's fate to settle down and raise a family once he's had a chance to sow his wild oats.

APOLLODORUS

Married people like to say things like that to scare single people, but I'm sure I can take some comfort in the fact that it would be hard to find another Xanthippe.

She's quite a prize.

SOCRATES

Not so hard as you might wish, perhaps. It's true that Xanthippe has more of the fury in her than most, but I think there's a lot of Xanthippe in all women.

But Xanthippe does deserve credit for this—she has been an exemplary wife in one respect: She has definitely helped steel me against any possible form of adversity life could offer.

But let's leave Xanthippe to scrubbing the floor or whatever else she may be doing to prepare herself for tomorrow, and turn our attention to the proposed topic of our nice little after dinner chat.

I believe, gentlemen, you know the procedure by now. To prevent me from just flying off on a wild tangent somewhere, I would like to ask a few questions to make sure we all agree on a couple of basic points before I really go off the deep end.

GROUP

Certainly!

SOCRATES

I'm glad to find you all so cooperative.

Zenas—if you will be so kind as to help us all find our way on this difficult subject—let us first investigate Aristophanes' contention that marriage is a kind of love.

Do you believe, along with our esteemed poet here, that love and marriage are one and the same thing, or are they two different things?

ZENAS

Two very different things I should say, Socrates, since it appears that we often find one without the other. In fact, they often seem to be as unlike as any two things can be.

SOCRATES

Ha—very good. Clearly, if we are to arrive at the truth in this matter, we must first consider what are the general types of love and marriage, and then we must further examine each in turn to try to determine what, if anything, it is that these all have in common, so that we can try to identify the true nature of love.

Don't you agree?

ZENAS

Yes, of course

SOCRATES

Then let us begin. First, what are the kinds of love?

ZENAS

Well, first, of course, there's love of family, as in the love you feel for your mother and father and sisters and brothers.

APOLLODORUS

Even if you hate them and want to kill them.

ZENAS

(ignoring him)

And there's love of friends. Then there's love of men and women you aren't related to and aren't friends with, or ....

APOLLODORUS

Now you're getting to the good part, Zenas.

ARISTOPHANES

Don't forget the kind of love someone feels for their pets, or the kind of love a farmer feels for the animals on his farm.

ZENAS

That's not love—that's sickness!

ARISTOPHANES

And doesn't love in general often strike you as being a kind of malady or sickness?

SOCRATES

So, Aristophanes, since you seem to have taken over for young Zenas here, what pray tell, then, are the kinds of marriage—unless there's anything you'd like to add, Zenas?

ZENAS

No, that just about covers it.

ARISTOPHANES

It's widely know that there are two kinds of marriage— bad and worse.

SOCRATES

And do you agree, Zenas?

ZENAS

Well, truly, Socrates, from all I see and hear, I would say it doesn't appear to be far from the truth.

APOLLODORUS

Upon that note, gentlemen, I would like to propose a toast—to Xanthippe!

GROUP

To Xanthippe!

SOCRATES

And so, gentlemen, now that we have determined what are the various forms of love and marriage, is there anything we can ascertain they have in common, which will help us come to an understanding of the true nature of love?

ARISTOPHANES

Why, even a fool could see that it's so obvious—misery!

SCENE VII

(Town center of Athens. Socrates and Xanthippe stand on a platform. Alcibiades is standing off to one side, looking up at Socrates, and Morona is standing off to the other side by Xanthippe.)

ALCIBIADES

Make sure you put her in her place, Socrates. I've thought Xanthippe's needed to be taken down a peg or two for a while now. We don't want these broads to start getting any funny ideas.

(goes to his seat)

MORONA

All of us woman are counting on you, Xanthippe. Don't let us down. Our husbands will never let us forget it if you let him get the better of you.

XANTHIPPE

Thanks, that really takes the pressure off.

MORONA

You'll do fine! Remember what we talked about yesterday.

And if that doesn't help—if you start to feel yourself get tongue-tied or need inspiration—just think of what your life would have been like if you had married a rich man who spoiled you rotten.

XANTHIPPE

Maybe I should forget the debate and just kill him.

MORONA

Perfect—that's what I want to hear. Break a leg—preferably his!

(goes to her seat)

MODERATOR

Ladies and gentlemen, we are gathered here today for a very special event.

No, this man, Socrates, and this woman, Xanthippe, are not here to join together in heavenly matrimony—They've already experienced that joy and are now years past that day of happiness, I can assure you.

Instead, you are about to witness a very remarkable and unparalleled occurrence in our history. For the first time ever in our illustrious city, a husband and wife are going to debate some of the greatest philosophical issues of all time.

They each have much at stake in this contest. Socrates, one of our most famous philosophers, has agreed that if he loses, he will forever renounce philosophizing within the walls of this city.

(At this point there is some intermingled clapping and booing distributed randomly throughout the audience and a few shouts of "damn philosopher.")

And Xanthippe has agreed that if she loses, she will... er ... stop nagging her husband to death.

(Again some booing and cheering, this time with some loud laughter and shouts of "Way to go Xanthippe!" thrown in.)

These are the terms that you have both earlier agreed to. With the people of Athens as witnesses, I ask you now to both affirm your willingness to be bound by the judgment of the majority decision of those present.

Do you both agree to let the citizens of Athens chose the winner of this competition and adhere to the rules of conduct governing you if you should lose?

BOTH

I do.

MODERATOR

Very well, then, let's get started. There will be at least two, and possibly three, topics for debate. The first two will be: "The one and the many" and "being and becoming."

If necessary, there will be a third topic, a tiebreaker on "the value of the philosophic life." Socrates won the drawing of lots that was held earlier to decide who gets to speak first, and thus he will begin.

Socrates, are you ready?

SOCRATES

I certainly am, my fine sir. But, with your permission, I would like to ask for assistance from someone here in our audience.

My friends know it is a habit of mine to always ask their help in arriving at the truth in our discussions, and so, if you don't mind, I would like to ask Zenas here if he would be willing to answer a few questions.

MODERATOR

By all means, Socrates.

XANTHIPPE

Why can't you ever just give a straight answer? Why do you always have to have someone else do your dirty work!

MODERATOR

Xanthippe, please wait your turn.

SOCRATES

As I was saying, it is customary for me to start out by asking a few preliminary questions of my admirers.

Zenas, would you be willing to give me a hand?

ZENAS

Of course, Socrates. Please feel free to ask me whatever you want and I'll do my best to try to answer it.

SOCRATES

Very well, then. First, do you agree that the one and the many are two separate things—that is, that there is the one and there is the many.

ZENAS

Yes, of course.

SOCRATES

That is, they are not the same.

ZENAS

Yes, yes—you're right.
(gushing, turns to Apollodorus)
I told you he's a genius!

APOLLODORUS

That's obvious.

SOCRATES

But, if they are not the same, then they are alike in that they are both different, so they are nonetheless the same, though different.

ZENAS

(excited)

Yes, yes—that's all true! I'll be damned if I understand a word of it—but I know you're right!

SOCRATES

Good, I'm glad you agree. You always were one of my better pupils— along with Alcibiades over there.

(He smiles and winks at Alcibiades, who nods.)

Now, on the other hand, the one is one, which is why we call it one. But the many, is more than one, which likewise is why we call it the more than one, or the many. Isn't that so?

ZENAS

Yes, ever single word of it—true as true can be.

SOCRATES

All right. But if the one is only one and the many is more than one, then the one is less than the many and different from it.

APOLLODORUS

(to Zenas)

I thought we already covered that part.

ZENAS

(under his breath)

Shut up!

SOCRATES

But if the one is less than the many, then the one is also a part of the many, which means they are the same.

Which brings us back to the same conclusion: The one and the many are both the same and different.

ZENAS

What did I tell you—an absolute genius, I say! There never was a wiser man!

(The audience claps and cheers for the most part, with a few hisses and boo's thrown in.)

APOLLODORUS

I'm beginning to understand what you mean when you say all he knows is that he knows nothing.

MODERATOR

That was a very impressive argument, Socrates. I think it is clear to all of us now, why it is that you have—justly—earned a reputation for your great wisdom, sir. It will, indeed, be a tough act for Xanthippe to follow.

All right, now. Xanthippe, it is now your turn to speak on "the one and the many". Are you ready?

XANTHIPPE

Yes, I am.

(falters)

The one and the many. Hmmmm ....

(pause, some laughter)

MODERATOR

All right everyone, now let's give her some time

MORONA

Come on, Xanthippe. Remember the strategy!

XANTHIPPE

(suddenly comes to life)

All right, you want to know about the one and the many—I'll tell you about the one and the many!

My husband has gone and stayed out all night at ONE damn party too MANY. I'm tired of barely having ONE bite to eat at the dinner table every night for the kids and me while he is off gorging himself at another of his MANY gourmet feasts. And he doesn't even bring us a doggy bag!

In short, I think I have ONE worthless husband too MANY—and I've been married ONE damn time too MANY!

(Laughter and applause. The women, especially, scream "You tell 'em, Xanthippe!")

MORONA

That's the way, Xanthippe ... Keep it up! Let him have it good!

MODERATOR

All right, that's a very strong show up support for your first response, Xanthippe. The people of Athens have clearly chosen you as the victor for the first question.

But there is still our second topic, being and becoming. Socrates, again, will speak first. Whenever you're ready, sir.

APOLLODORUS

Looks as though your friend might be in some trouble.

ZENAS

No way!

SOCRATES

Once again I would like to ask whether Zenas would be willing to help me by agreeing to—I mean answering—a few questions.

ZENAS

It would be an honor Socrates.

SOCRATES

Thank you. Let's get started then, shall we?

There is a difference between being something and becoming something, don't you agree? A man is a certain age—but he is becoming another age at the same time.

So he is simultaneously being and becoming.

ZENAS

Yes.

SOCRATES

Now, then, if a man is being and becoming at the same time—then he can never BE anything because he is always BECOMING something else.

ZENAS

Yes.

SOCRATES

But, then again, he can never BECOME anything else if he never IS something to begin with, isn't that so?

ZENAS

Yes, every damn word of it!

SOCRATES

Therefore, a man is both being and becoming and not being and becoming at the same time. The audience cheers and claps, with some booing thrown in.

ZENAS

A prodigy—if ever there was one!

APOLLODORUS

I say we string this guy up from the nearest available tree. Then he'll have a pretty good idea of what he is and what he's becoming.

(Zenas ignores him amidst all the clapping and cheering.)

MODERATOR

Well, you seemed to have made quite a comeback, Socrates. Xanthippe, it's your turn again now. What do you have to say on the subject of being and becoming?

XANTHIPPE

Plenty! (loudly) I'm tired of BEING made a fool of by my damn husband. I AM mad, and I'm BECOMING madder! I'm sick and tired of living in a hovel while he's off living the good life all the time with his rich friends. I AM tired of the no good bum and I'm sick of putting up with his damn philosophizing!

If you don't shape up, old man, and stop loafing around all over town all day and start supporting your family, I'm going to stop BEING so damn nice to you, and I'm going to BECOME violent. To conclude, your time of BEING is short, and if you keep up your damn philosophy nonsense, you are about to BECOME history!

You like to keep those damn gums flapping in the breeze. This will help wet your whistle.

(She picks up a pitcher of water on the podium and pours it over his head.)

(Everyone laughs uproariously—and the audience cheers her on overwhelmingly.)

SOCRATES

First Xanthippe thunders, then she pours.

MODERATOR

I think it's fair to say it's unanimous. There is clearly no need for a discussion of the merits of the philosophical life to decide the question.

Xanthippe, I hereby declare you the winner of this debate, and, Socrates, I hereby notify you that from this day forward you are forever banned from in any way practicing philosophy within the city of Athens.

SOCRATES

But it's not fair—I was just getting warmed up!

In the next part I was going to get into a no holds barred discussion of 'the good' and 'the bad'—that's my specialty!

XANTHIPPE

I'll tell you what's not fair—making your family the victims of your damn hypocrisy.

You may do wonders for all the idle young drunks in this city—but you don't do anything for your kids and me.

But the party's over, buddy. You've had your fun. Now we're going to get you a job!

(Xanthippe grabs him and pulls him offstage.)

SOCRATES

Help!